Caillou®

Meets Sophie

A Story About Autism

**An initiative
of Sophie Desmarais**

Jasmin Roy
Sophie Desmarais
FOUNDATION
Creators of a caring environment

Text: Kim Thompson
Illustrations: Mario Allard
Content validation and poster: Autism Canada

chouette   dhx media®   AUTISM CANADA
SEE THE SPECTRUM
DIFFERENTLY

Caillou was at the park with Rosie and Grandma. He saw a little girl playing all by herself.
"I'm going to ask that girl if she wants to play with me," he told Grandma.
"What a good idea!" replied Grandma. "Maybe you will make a new friend today."

"Hello!" said Caillou.
The girl didn't answer, so he spoke a little louder.
"My name is Caillou," he said. "Do you want to play with me?"
The girl just sat there. Caillou was confused. Did she hear him? Was she shy? Should he leave her alone?
Caillou didn't know what to do.

Some children were playing tag nearby. They were laughing and shouting. It looked like fun. Caillou wondered if the girl would like to join them, but she seemed very unhappy. "What's wrong?" he asked, but she didn't answer. Instead, she got up and ran away.

The girl hid under a picnic table. Caillou wondered
if she needed help. Then a man walked up.
"Hello," he said. "That's Sophie, and I'm her dad."
"Is she all right?" asked Caillou.
"Yes. She just needs to calm down. This will help."
He handed Sophie a little toy.
"Let's give her a little space," he said to Caillou.

"Why is she upset?" asked Caillou.
"Sophie doesn't like loud noises," explained her dad.
"She has autism, so she sometimes acts a little different than other kids. She doesn't talk very much."
"She didn't talk to me," said Caillou.
"She's like that with everyone, even me. And when something bothers her, she likes to sit somewhere quiet and dark."

Soon Sophie came out and went back to the fountain.
Caillou wanted to join her.
"Can I sit with Sophie?" he asked her dad. "I promise
I won't be noisy."
"Yes, she would like that
very much," said Sophie's dad.
"Even if she doesn't say so."

Caillou sat beside Sophie. She was looking at the fountain so he decided to look at it too. "Wow!" he whispered.
The drops of water sparkled like jewels in the sunlight. Now Caillou understood why Sophie liked to watch the water falling. It was beautiful.

Sophie put her hand into the water, so Caillou did too. The water was nice and cool. Then Sophie laughed.

"What's so funny?" asked Caillou. Then he noticed the waves made his hand look wobbly and funny. He started to laugh too.

"Hand!" said Sophie, giggling.

"Hand!" said Caillou.

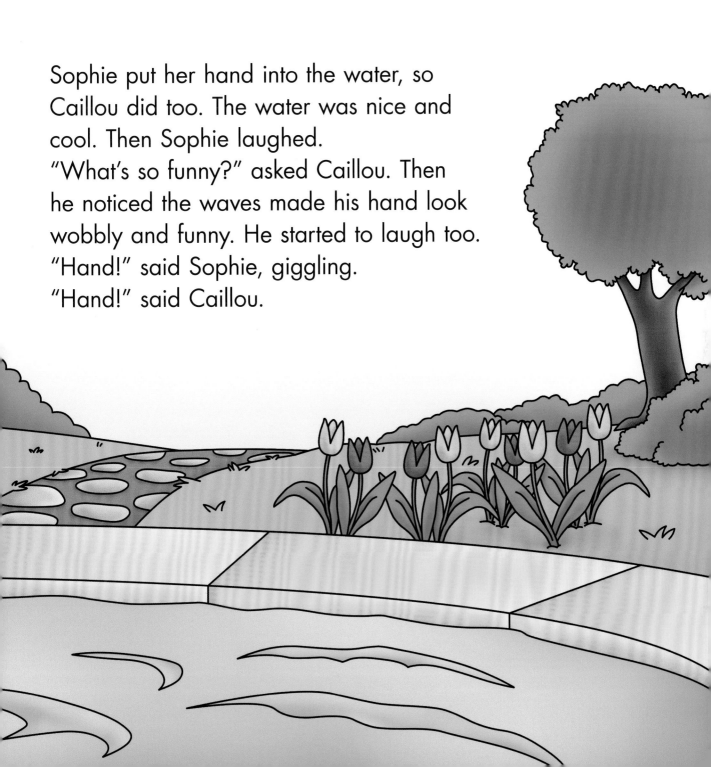

Then the loud children ran past them again. Caillou saw Sophie frown. He knew she didn't like the noise they were making.

"Shhh!" he said to the kids, but they didn't hear him.

Caillou didn't want Sophie to be upset. He wondered what he could do to make her feel better.

Then Caillou remembered something that would help.
He picked up Sophie's little toy and gave it to her.
"Here, Sophie," he said.
She held it to her cheek and took a deep breath. Then
she smiled. Caillou could see that she was feeling better.
He was glad he could help.

Soon it was time to go home.
"Who is your new friend?" asked Grandma.
"That's Sophie," said Caillou. "She has autism. She
doesn't say very much, but she notices lots of things."
Caillou waved goodbye to Sophie.
She didn't wave back, but she smiled
at him. That made Caillou very happy.

Sophie has autism, but it doesn't
prevent her from having fun like
any other little boy or girl.

Text by Kim Thompson
All rights reserved.
Illustrations: Mario Allard
Coloration: Eric Lehouillier

The PBS KIDS logo is a registered mark of PBS and is used with permission.

Chouette Publishing would like to thank the Government of Canada and SODEC
for their financial support.

Books
Tax Credit

Gestion
SODEC

Bibliothèque et Archives nationales du Québec and Library and Archives
Canada cataloguing in publication

Thompson, Kim, 1964-, author

Caillou meets Sophie: a story about autism/text, Kim Thompson; illustrations,
Mario Allard.

Target audience: For children aged 3 and up.

ISBN 978-2-89718-505-3 (softcover)

1. Caillou (Fictitious character) - Juvenile literature. 2. Autism in children -
Juvenile literature. 3. Autistic children - Juvenile literature. I. Allard, Mario,
1969-, illustrator. II. Title.

RJ506.A9T46 2019   j618.92'85882   C2018-942712-4

Printed in China
10 9 8 7 6 5 4 3 2 1 CHO2047 NOV2018

...y sometimes understand
...when you use pictures
...ain it.

...eaning is clear and
...–pictures too.

Kids who have autism may struggle to recognize
emotion in other people, but they have feelings,
just like you do.

**Take the time to explain what you're feeling and
take time to let them explain what they're feeling.**

...on't like disturbances,
...lden movements.

...ns and respect their need
...meout in a calm place.

Kids who have autism like to have fun
and make friends, just like other kids do.

**Help them feel included by sharing activities
with them.**

...lopmental disorder. ...use it isn't a sickness.

...tism, invite them to play **part of the group.**

Kids who have autism like routine and organization. It soothes them.

Respect their habits and routines.

...ne advice to help you make friends with the kids in your group who have autism.

...ies noise. Also, Sophie ..., ... her routine: When she goes to the park, she always sits in the same place, right beside the fountain.

A message from Sophie's dad:

Sophie is happy when someone plays with her, even if she doesn't say so. Like all kids, she loves to have fun, to make friends, and to discover the world around her. If you know a kid with autism, invite them to play and help them feel a part of the group. You may learn a lot from them!

Illustrations: Mario Allard

Hand!

Kids who have autism ma... something more quickly ... to expl...

Use words whose m...
—if it's helpful-

Some kids with autism ... loud noises, or su...

Be sensitive to their reactio...
to occasionally take a ti...

Caillou®

Autism is a neurodeve
It isn't contagious, becc

**If you know a kid with au
and help them feel a**

Hi there! I wanted to introduce you to my friend Sophie.

She has autism. That means that her brain works differently than the brain of someone who doesn't have autism. For example, she has trouble communicating with people. She ha͟tes ͟ ͟ ͟ ͟ ͟ ͟ ͟ ͟ ͟ ͟ ͟ ͟ ͟ ͟ ie really likes